MY UNCLE PODGER

A PICTURE BOOK

Created by Wallace Tripp

BASED ON A PASSAGE FROM
THREE MEN IN A BOAT
(TO SAY NOTHING OF THE DOG)
BY
JEROME K. JEROME

LITTLE, BROWN AND COMPANY
BOSTON   TORONTO

Picture books by Wallace Tripp

A GREAT BIG UGLY MAN CAME UP AND TIED HIS HORSE TO ME
MY UNCLE PODGER

FIRST EDITION

T 06/75

An edited version of the text and selected artwork from this book
appeared in the May 1975 issue of CRICKET magazine

LIBRARY OF CONGRESS CATALOGING IN PUBLICATION DATA

Tripp, Wallace.
  My Uncle Podger.

  SUMMARY: Instructing everyone to leave such a
simple little thing to him, Uncle Podger attempts to
hang a picture, creating general chaos in the process.
  [1. Humorous stories] I. Jerome, Jerome Klapka,
1859-1927. Three men in a boat. II. Title.
PZ7.T7364My   [E]   74-19040
ISBN 0-316-46180-6

Published simultaneously in Canada
by Little, Brown & Company (Canada) Limited

PRINTED IN THE UNITED STATES OF AMERICA

For My Aunt Cap

You never saw such a commotion up and down a house, in all your life, as when my Uncle Podger undertook to do a job.

One day a picture came home from the framemaker's, and was standing in the dining room, waiting to be put up; and when Aunt Podger asked what was to be done with it, Uncle Podger said:

"Oh, you leave that to me. Don't you, any of you, worry yourselves about that. I'll do all that."

And then he took off his coat, and began. He sent the girl out for sixpen'orth of nails, and then one of the boys after her to tell her what size to get; and, from that, he gradually worked down, and started the whole house.

"Now you go and get me my hammer, Will," he shouted; "and you bring me the rule, Tom; and I shall want the stepladder, and I had better have a kitchen chair, too; and, Jim! you run round to Mr. Goggles, and tell him, 'Pa's kind regards, and hopes his leg's better; and will he lend him his spirit level?' And don't you go, Maria, because I shall want somebody to hold me the light; and when the girl comes back, she must go out again for a bit of picture cord; and Tom!—where's Tom?—Tom, you come here; I shall want you to hand me up the picture."

And then he lifted up the picture, and dropped it, and it came out of the frame, and

he tried to save the glass, and cut himself;

and then he sprang round the room, looking
for his handkerchief. He could not find his
handkerchief, because it was in the pocket of
the coat he had taken off, and he did not know

10

where he had put the coat, and all the house
had to leave off looking for his tools, and
start looking for his coat; while he danced
round and hindered them.

11

"Doesn't anybody in the whole house know
where my coat is? I never came across such
a set in all my life—upon my word I didn't.
Six of you!—and you can't find a coat that I
put down not five minutes ago! Well, of all
the—"

Then he got up, and found that he had been sitting on it, and called out:

"Oh, you can give it up! I've found it myself now. Might just as well ask the cat to find anything as expect you people to find it."

And, when half an hour had been spent in
tying up his finger, and a new glass had been
got, and the tools, and the ladder, and the
chair, and the candle had been brought, he
had another go, with the whole family, includ-
ing the girl and the charwoman, standing
round in a semicircle, ready to help. Two
people had to hold the chair, and a third helped

14

him up on it, and held him there, and a fourth handed him a nail, and a fifth passed him up the hammer, and he took hold of the nail, and dropped it.

"There!" he said in an injured tone, "now the nail's gone."

And we all had to go down on our knees and grovel for it, while he stood on the chair, and grunted, and wanted to know if he was to be kept tnere all the evening.

The nail was found at last, but by that time he had lost the hammer.

"Where's the hammer? What did I do with the hammer? Great heavens! Seven of you, gaping round there, and you don't know what I did with the hammer!"

We found the hammer for him, and then
he had lost sight of the mark he had made on
the wall, where the nail was to go in, and each
of us had to get up on the chair, beside him,
and see if we could find it; and we each dis-
covered it in a different place, and he called

us all fools, one after another, and told us to get down. And he took the rule, and re-measured, and found that he wanted half thirty-one and three-eighths inches from the corner, and tried to do it in his head, and went mad.

And we all tried to do it in our heads, and all arrived at different results, and sneered at one another. And in the general row, the original number was forgotten, and Uncle Podger had to measure it again.

He used a bit of string this time, and at the critical moment, when the old fool was leaning over the chair at an angle of forty-five, and trying to reach a point three inches beyond what was possible for him to reach, the string slipped, and down he slid onto the

piano, a really fine musical effect being produced by the suddenness with which his head and body struck all the notes at the same time.

And Aunt Maria said that she would not allow the children to stand round and hear such language.

At last, Uncle Podger got the spot fixed again, and put the point of the nail on it with his left hand, and took the hammer in his right hand. And with the first blow, he smashed his thumb, and dropped the hammer, with a yell, on somebody's toes.

Aunt Maria mildly observed that, next time Uncle Podger was going to hammer a nail into the wall, she hoped he'd let her know in time, so that she could make arrangements to go and spend a week with her mother while it was being done.

"Oh! you women, you make such a fuss over everything," Uncle Podger replied, picking himself up. "Why, I like doing a little job of this sort."

And then he had another try, and, at the
second blow, the nail went clean through the
plaster, and half the hammer after it, and
Uncle Podger was precipitated against the
wall with force nearly sufficient to flatten
his nose.

Then we had to find the rule and the string again, and a new hole was made; and, about midnight, the picture was up — very crooked and insecure, the wall for yards round looking as if it had been smoothed down with a rake, and everybody dead beat and wretched — except Uncle Podger.

"There you are," he said, stepping heavily off the chair onto the charwoman's corns, and surveying the mess he had made with evident pride. "Why, some people would have had a man in to do a little thing like that!"

AFTERWORD

Jerome K. Jerome (1859–1927), English humorist and playwright, was born in Staffordshire and grew up in London. After terminating his schooling at age fourteen, he rattled about, railroad clerking, reading in the British Museum, touring with a theatrical company, reporting and teaching. Favorable reception of his column, "Idle Thoughts of an Idle Fellow," led him into journalism and editing. Costs in a lawsuit eventually forced Jerome to abandon the two newspapers he had built up and he turned to playwriting, at which he was a success. The Passing of the Third Floor Back was particularly popular and ran for seven years.

In 1889, when he was thirty, Jerome wrote Three Men in a Boat (to Say Nothing of the Dog), a hilarious account of a boating trip on the Thames by three of literature's greatest bumbling twits (to say nothing of Montmorency, their immortal fox terrier). The book is a minor classic of English fiction.

MY UNCLE PODGER (drawn from the third chapter of Three Men in a Boat) is in its original context the narrator's comparison of one of his traveling companions to an extraordinary relative. For simplicity and clarity a slight adjustment has been made in Jerome's use of tenses; otherwise the text is in all essentials just as Jerome wrote it, in the certainty that it could not be improved upon.

W.T.